The Cloak

Garfield's Apprentices

Already published

In preparation

LEON GARFIELD

The Cloak

Illustrated by
FAITH JAQUES

HEINEMANN
London

William Heinemann Ltd
15 Queen Street, Mayfair, London W1X 8BE

LONDON   MELBOURNE   TORONTO
JOHANNESBURG   AUCKLAND

To Vivien

First published 1976
© Leon Garfield 1976
Illustrations © Faith Jaques 1976

434 94034 8

Printed and bound in Great Britain by
Morrison & Gibb Ltd., London and Edinburgh

It was New Year's morning and nature, in a burst of good resolutions, had decided to begin with a clean slate —or about a million of them: snow had fallen heavily during the night. Everything was white; roofs, alleys, courts, lanes and streets looked as fresh and hopeful as a clean page awaiting the first entry. . . .

A greasy old lamplighter, high on his ladder in Southampton Street, brooded on it all. He saw his own footprints and the marks made by his heavy ladder as he'd moved from lamp to lamp. Everything showed; even where he'd stumbled. He saw two kitchen maids hastening to fetch the morning's milk. He wished them a happy new year, and his voice, floating down through the silence imposed by the snow, startled them. They looked up with bright morning faces, wagged their fingers at the old man and laughingly returned his greeting.

The silence was uncanny; folk moved across the white like toiling dreams. A gipsy woman with a laden donkey came down from Covent Garden way as soundlessly as a black thought.

5

Her face was dark, her hair was wild and she and her beast trudged up a little storm in the snow.

"Apples! Sweet Kent apples!" she cried as she saw the lamplighter. "Who'll buy?"

She halted beside the ladder and turned her fierce eyes upward.

"No teeth," said the lamplighter sadly. He gazed down and into the baskets the donkey patiently bore. In one lay a bushel of green and yellow apples; in the other, well wrapped in rags, slept a tiny baby, no more than a week old. The lamplighter grinned.

"But I must say, your little 'un looks soft enough to eat . . . even with poor, bare gums like these."

He stretched back his lips in a kindly snarl.

"You can have her for a pound," said the gipsy.

"Nowhere to put her, dear."

"Fifteen shillings, then? Just so long as she goes to a good home."

The lamplighter shook his head. He climbed down from his perch and, dipping his little finger into a tin of blacking he'd been gathering from the burnt remains of his lamps, reached into the basket and marked the top of the baby's head with a tiny cross.

"That's for luck, dear. Lamplighter's blacking; nought shall be lacking."

"That's kind," said the gipsy approvingly. "Here's a sprig of white heather for you and yours. Gipsy's heather brings good weather. Where's the nearest pawnshop?"

"That's a bad way to start the new year, dear," said the old man.

6

"Got to keep body and soul together," countered the gipsy. "Ain't I?"

The lamplighter scratched his head as he considered the problem.

"They won't take apples . . . nor babies, neither."

"Got a garment," said the woman proudly.

"They'll take that. Right off your back, if need be."

"Will they?"

She stared into the lamplighter's cracked and ancient eyes. Suddenly he kindled up and grinned with an air of elderly mischief.

"Drury Lane, dear. Mr Thompson's."

The gipsy returned the old man's smile.

"Rachel's blessing on you!" she called as she began to continue on her way.

"And a happy New Year!" answered the lamplighter, watching the woman and her donkey move soundlessly down the street, kicking up the snow in a fine spray so that it seemed they were walking upon a long white sea. It was just five minutes to eight o'clock.

At the southern end of Drury Lane, upon the left-hand side, stood the premises of Mr Thompson, Personal Banking on Moderate Terms. From a stout iron gibbet above the shop door hung the emblems of the trade: three brass balls that winked and gleamed in the wintry sunshine, beckoning to all in distress. Even on them the snow had settled, crowning them with caps of white so that they resembled three little round and shining brides of Christ.

Upon closer examination the brass balls did indeed
bear vague smudges like countenances, but not of a
particularly radiant cast. Long ago, an actor (most of
Mr Thompson's customers were on the stage, or tempor-
arily off it) had climbed up and painted the masks of
grim Tragedy on each of them; but time, weather, and the
scrubbing brush of Coot, the apprentice, had worn them
away to the merest ghosts of grief.

A rigid man, was Mr Thompson (and so was his brother-
in-law, Mr Long, who pawnbroked in nearby Henrietta
Street), and he conducted his business on the principle of
the iron hand in the iron glove.

"A pawner is a man in difficulties," he always warned his apprentice whenever he was called away and had to leave the shop in that youth's care. "And a man in difficulties is a man in despair. Now despair, my boy, makes a man untrustworthy; it turns him into a liar, a swindler, a cheat. Poverty may not be a crime; but in my experience it's the cause of most of 'em. Poverty debases a man; and a base man is a man to keep a sharp eye on. It tells us in the Bible that it's hard enough for a rich man to enter the Kingdom of Heaven; so think how much harder it is for a poor one and the dishonest things he'll do to get there! He'll swear on his mother's grave that the article he's pawning is worth twice as much as ever we could sell it for. He'll give you his solemn word that it's only a loan and that he'll come back tomorrow and redeem it. We know those redeemers, my boy. Like tomorrow, they never come. So you watch out!"

With these words Mr Thompson had left his apprentice as he and his brother-in-law, Mr Long, had gone off into the country for Christmas and the New Year. Then, recollecting that it was a festive season, had thought a joke to be in order.

"And if anyone comes," he added, with a grisly twinkle in his eye, "and wants to pawn a soul, you just send him down to Mr Long's! A merry Christmas, my boy; and if you watch out, a prosperous New Year!"

Accordingly the apprentice watched out; he watched out in ways, perhaps, that even his master never suspected.

He was a neat, thin youth of sixteen and was in the fourth year of his apprenticeship. He wore brass-rimmed spectacles (borrowed from stock), which lent him a studious air and enlarged his eyes which were, otherwise, inclined to be small and furtive.

Although the shop was not yet open, he was already seated on his high stool in a discreet wooden cubby-hole that resembled a confessional, occupied in resting his elbows on the counter and making mysterious entries in a ledger. Beside him was a short piece of mahogany on which his name—Mister Coot—was painted in black; and beside that was a yellowed card announcing that: "The House of Thompson wishes all its customers a Happy New Year". It was kept in a small linen wallet and brought out every year.

Presently, having completed his entries, Coot gazed at the festive card and, with a jerk of inspiration, arranged the piece of mahogany over it to produce the heart-warming sentiment that, "The House of Thompson wishes Mister Coot a Happy New Year".

He sat for several minutes admiring it, then fished in his waistcoat pocket and came up with a massive silver watch secured to his person by means of a stout steel chain, like a criminal. He flicked up the lid and, observing that it lacked a minute till opening time, he thoughtfully picked his nose. At eight o'clock, Coot-time, he slipped from his stool, crawled under the counter and unbolted the door, returning with rat-like speed and dexterity lest a customer should catch him at a disadvantage. The House of Thompson was open to the new year.

The first customer was an ageing actor, hoping to raise five shillings on a pair of breeches not worth three.

"And—and a happy New Year to you!" he finished up, leaning over the counter with a mixture of affability and confidence through which despair showed in patches.

Coot smiled his pawnbroker's smile (which was next door to an undertaker's), and silently removed his name from the card, thereby returning the greeting and saving his breath.

He began to examine the breeches with fastidious care.

"Did I leave a guinea in it, old boy?" he asked with pathetic jocularity as Coot turned out the pocket.

Coot said nothing; he was watching out. He pushed the breeches back to their owner.

"Ay'm afraid they ain't much use to us. A bit too far gone."

The actor was thunderstruck. He was outraged; he was humiliated; he was bitterly dismayed. He argued, he pleaded, he begged—

"All right. A shillin', then," interposed Coot composedly, when he judged the customer to be sufficiently low in spirits to be agreeable to anything.

"A shilling? But—"

"Try Mr Long's in 'enrietta Street. P'raps my colleague, Mister Jeremiah Snipe, might up me a penny or two. On the other 'and, 'e might down me a sixpence. Go on. Shove off and try Mister Jeremiah."

The pawnbroker's apprentice stared coolly at the customer, knowing him to be a beaten man. He wouldn't try Jeremiah—never in a month of Sundays! He wouldn't dare risk another such slap in the face. He was done for; he didn't even kick up much of a fuss when tuppence was knocked off his shilling: a penny for receipt and warehousing and a penny for two months' interest in advance.

"Really," he muttered. "That's a bit sharp, ain't it?"

For answer, Coot slid his eyes towards two framed notices that hung on the cubby-hole's wall. Decorated with the emblems of the trade, in the manner of illuminated missals, they set forth the rates of interest permitted by law, and the regulations designed to protect both parties, in a lending transaction, from the sharp practice of each other.

Wearily the actor shook his head. There was no sense in wasting his eyesight on the small print. Everything was above board, and the apprentice was as honest as an iron bar.

"I'll be back next week," he said, taking his tenpence and mournfully patting his pawned garment, "to redeem you, old friend."

"Redeem? You don't know the meanin' of the word,"

murmured Coot, as the customer departed into the not quite new year.

Next came a fellow trying to pawn a wig, but the watchful apprentice found lice in it and sent him packing; and after him came a lady with the odd request that the apprentice should turn his back while she took off her petticoat hoops on which she wanted to borrow seven shillings.

"Turn me back?" said Coot, mindful of Mr Thompson's instruction to watch out. "Ay'm afraid not. You might even nick me timepiece," he said, laying that precious object (which his father had given him to mark the beginning of his apprenticeship) on the counter. "I'll just sit as I am and not put temptation in your way."

So the lady, with abject blushings, was forced to display her dirty linen and torn stockings to Coot's dreadful smile.

"Why—they ain't even real whalebone," he said, when the hoops were offered across the counter. "Ay'm afraid they ain't much use to us. Two shillin's. That's the best."

"You dirty little skinflint!"

"Come to think on it," said Coot, rightly taking the expression as a personal insult, "a shillin' and ninepence is nearer the mark."

He pushed the hoops back. "Or you can try Mr Long's in 'enrietta Street. My colleague, Mister Jeremiah Snipe, might up me a penny or two. On the other 'and, 'e might down me a sixpence. Go on. Shove off and try Mister Jeremiah."

He stared at her trembling lips and tear-filled eyes. She'd not try Jeremiah—never in a month of Sundays!

15

He was right, of course; he was always right; that was why Mr Thompson trusted him.

"I'll be back, of course," said the lady, struggling to salvage some shreds of her self-respect, "to redeem them next week."

With that, she snatched up her shilling and ninepence (less tuppence), and departed into the fast-ageing year.

Coot smiled and watched her through the window, noticing how her unsupported skirts dragged in the snow and wiped out her footprints even as she made them.

"Redeem?" he murmured. "You don't know the meanin' of the word!"

He sat still for a moment, lost in philosophy; then he slipped from his stool, crawled under the counter and bolted the street door. Returning, he gathered up the hoops and breeches, ticketed them and carried them into the warehousing room at the back of the shop.

Here, in a dispiriting gloom that smelled of fallen fortunes, humbled pride and camphor to keep off the moth, they took their places amidst a melancholy multitude of pledges awaiting redemption. Wigs, coats, gowns and sheets, walking-sticks, wedding rings, shoes and watches waited in a long and doleful queue as, month by month, they were moved up till, at the end of a year and a day, they were sold off, unredeemed.

It was a grim sight; but Coot, being in the trade, was not unduly moved by it. He surveyed the crowded racks and pigeon-holes and shelves.

"Redeemed?" he whispered. "You don't know the meanin' of the word!"

When he arrived back, he found his cubby-hole as black
as night; in his absence, a shadow, thick as a customer,
seemed to have taken up residence.

"What the 'ell—" began the apprentice; then, craning
his neck, he saw the gipsy woman at the window, obscuring
the light.

She'd got her arms stretched out and was pressing her
face and hands against the dirty glass as if to see what was
being offered for sale. She gave Coot quite a turn, looming
up like that; angrily, he waved her off.

She grinned at him and pointed to the sign that hung

over the door. Coot frowned; of all folk, gipsies needed watching the most. Turn your back on them and they'd have the buttons off your coat.

"Shove off!" he mouthed. "And a 'orrible Noo Year!"

But the woman continued to grin, showing a set of teeth much too good for her. She pointed to the sign again and moved aside so that Coot could see her donkey. Vigorously he shook his head.

"No livestock!" he shouted. "Don't take 'em. Try Mr Long's in 'enrietta Street!"

Now it was the gipsy's turn to shake her head, so Coot unbolted the door and it opened by a crack. At once a sinewy brown hand came through and grasped the lintel. Coot glared at it and meditated slamming the door hard.

"Rachel's blessing on you, dear!" came the gipsy's harsh voice.

"Wotcher want?"

"Got something to pawn."

"Nicked?"

"You know better than to ask that, dear!"

He did indeed. Nevertheless he had to watch out. Come to think of it, there wasn't much time left for watching out; Mr Thompson was due back in a couple of days.

"What is it, then?"

"Garment."

Coot snorted. The gipsy stank like one o'clock. He'd not have advanced a sixpence on every stitch she stood up in—including whatever she wore underneath.

"Try Mr Long's in 'enrietta Street," he said, and tried to shut the door.

"Real silk, dear," said the gipsy. "Fur collar and all. Worth a mint."

Coot opened the door a further two inches and applied his eye to the gap, taking care to duck under the grasping hand. He saw that the woman was clutching a bundle under her free arm.

"That it?"

She laughed and tossed back a flap of the bundle. Coot saw the top of a baby's head. There was a black mark on it.

"Don't you bring that in 'ere," said Coot nervously. "It's got somethin' nasty."

"But it's cold out here."

"You should have thought on that before. You gipsies ain't fit to 'ave babies. It don't come in 'ere."

To Coot's surprise, the gipsy nodded meekly and returned the baby to its basket. Then she came back carrying a black article that she'd removed from one of the bundles on the donkey. It was silk, sure enough.

"All right," he said, letting go of the door and bolting back to his place with his customary neatness and speed. But as he settled on his stool, he couldn't help feeling that she'd been too quick for him and come in while he was still at a disadvantage.

Silently the garment was passed over the counter and Coot began to examine it. It was a cloak of black silk with a violet lining. The collar was real fox fur, and round the inside of the neck there was some delicate embroidery. It certainly was a handsome article; but nevertheless, the pawnbroker's apprentice knew he had to watch out.

"'ow did you come by it?"

"It was my father's, dear."

"Oh yes. Your father's." Coot grinned knowingly.

"My father's!" repeated the woman, with a touch of anger.

"Where are you from?" pursued Coot. "Got to ask on account of the law."

"Kent."

"That's a long way off."

"T'other side o' the moon!"

"Far enough, eh?" said Coot, meaningly.

The woman nodded. "Far enough, dear."

"'ow much was you expectin' on this garment?"

"Two silver pounds, dear."

"And the rest! D'you think I'm off me 'ead? Two pound to a thievin' old thing like you? You're 'avin' me on! Two pound for a bit of furry rubbish like this? Take a look at it . . . take a good look! Moth in the collar like nobody's business! And what about this stitchin'? Won't last out a week! And—and look 'ere! Dirty great stain that won't come out in a month of Sundays!" (There was indeed a rusty brown stain on the violet lining, though it was not a large one.) "And the 'ole garment whiffs something awful. Never get that smell off it! If I was to let you 'ave five shillin's on this, I'd be doin' you a favour and meself an injury."

"Only five shillings, dear? I was hoping, I was counting on more than that. I got my little one to care for."

"Like I said, my good woman, you should 'ave thought on that before. Five shillin's is the 'ouse's best."

"A pound, dear. Make it a silver pound!"

21

"Why don't you shove off? Try Mr Long's in 'enrietta
Street. Maybe my colleague, Mister Jeremiah, might up
me a penny or two. On the other 'and, 'e might down me
a sixpence. Go on. Shove off!"

"Ten shillings! Give me ten silver shillings!"

"Five. What would my master say if I was to give you
over the odds? 'e'd 'ave me out quicker'n a dose of rhubarb!
You want to do me down, you do! Five shillin's—or I send
for the constable!"

This was Coot's masterstroke. The woman's eyes
widened and she began to tremble. He'd got her!

"All right, then—all right!" she muttered. "Give me
the five silver shillings and a receipt."

"Receipt? What do you want that for?"

"To—to redeem my cloak. I—I'm coming back for it . . . soon."

"Redeem?" said Coot. "You don't know the meanin' of the word!"

But the gipsy insisted with all the obstinate ignorance of her tribe; so Coot chuckled and wrote out a receipt.

"That'll cost you another threepence," he said, giving her the money and packing her off out of the shop.

When she was safely out of sight, he bolted the door and examined the cloak again. He tried it on, but it was far too big for him, and covered him like a shroud. He tried lifting a corner and flinging it over his shoulder, in the manner of an ancient Roman; but it really wasn't his style. Regretfully he took it off, noticing that the rusty stain was on the left-hand side and would, had he been of a height, have covered his heart; as it was, it rested over his sweetbread. Thoughtfully he stroked the fur collar and looked again at the embroidery round the inside of the neck. He pursed his lips; then he grinned broadly. The embroidery was not, as he'd first supposed, a pattern; it was instead a line of Gothic letters making up a text.

"I KNOW THAT MY REDEEMER LIVETH," said the pawned cloak.

"That's what they all say!" chuckled the pawnbroker's apprentice. "But they don't know the meanin' of the word!"

By half past seven in the evening, the brave New Year was torn to tatters. No more snow had fallen and clean white streets were crossed and double-crossed by the black passing of men and women going about their daily affairs.

Freed from toil, the pawnbroker's apprentice chose to walk where the snow had been well trodden down. He was wearing his best shoes and did not want to spoil them; also, perhaps, at the back of his watchful mind was the thought that it was best to leave no footprints as his journey would not bear the closest examination.

He walked with a springy step, quite like a young lamb; it was as if all his hours of grimly patient dealing had compressed him like a spring, so that now he leaped forth with a youthful twang. He was done up to the nines, wearing a dazzling waistcoat, a ginger wig and silken breeches of egg-yolk yellow. He was a butterfly; he was a youth transformed.

Presently he reached Henrietta Street and gave a smart double knock on the door of Mr Long's (Loans Arranged on Modest Security): and while he waited, winked up knowingly at the three brass balls. J. Snipe opened the door.

"A 'appy Noo Year, Jerry!"

"Same to you, Cooty. And with three brass knobs on!"

Jeremiah, who was renowned for his wit, smirked as he stepped aside to admit his colleague and friend. He was a month younger than Coot and of a round-faced, angelic appearance that tended to make his customers feel ashamed of bargaining with him. But there lurked under that soft exterior a spirit every bit as stern as Coot's. Well, perhaps not quite so stern as he'd been in the trade four weeks less than his friend; but he was catching up fast.

"You've got something, haven't you, Cooty?"

Coot beamed.

"Thought so," said Jeremiah shrewdly. "That's why you're done up like the cat's dinner."

"Take a squint at this," said Coot, ignoring his colleague's wit. "Gipsy brought it."

He produced the cloak. Jeremiah whistled, then crawled under his counter so that he might examine the article from his usual situation. Coot made to follow him when he saw Jeremiah's boot defensively poised; so he stayed the wrong side of the counter reflecting that, whenever positions were reversed, he defended his own territory in the same way.

"Five pound," said Jeremiah, when he had finished studying the garment.

"Don't you come the skinflint with me, Jerry," said Coot affably. "Make it six."

Jeremiah smiled like an angel in a stained-glass window —a very stained-glass window—and nodded. "Six it is, then."

Agreement having been thus reached, the two industrious apprentices settled down to complete the necessary business of their interesting arrangement. As was required by law, Jeremiah noted down the transaction in Mr Long's ledger, while Coot did the same in his own ledger which had nothing to do with the law. Then Jeremiah handed over six pounds of Mr Long's money, less the cost of warehousing, receipting and two months' interest in advance; as was permitted by law. This done, Coot handed back to Jeremiah half of the proceeds, as was demanded by the terms of their partnership and the liability of their friendship.

"It's not as if we was thieves," Coot had said to Jeremiah when the idea had first come to him and Jeremiah had cast doubts on its honesty. "We're just business men. We ain't reely breakin' the law. You might say we ain't even goin' close enough to touch it! Look at it this way, Jerry," he'd gone on, feeling that his colleague remained unconvinced. "Think of bankers."

"Well?"

"They're lawful, ain't they?"

"According to their lights."

"Well, then—you put your money in a bank—"

"—I don't. I keep it in my shoe."

"I was just supposin'. You put your money in a bank,

and then the bank goes and does all sorts of things with it. Lends it out, invests it, buys things with it . . . and generally treats it like the money was its own. And that's what we'll be doin'. Folk pawn articles with us, and we pawn 'em again to each other. We're only borrerin' and lendin' out at interest. We ain't stealin', we're just re-investin'. And as long as nobody catches on, we'll end up in pocket. Bound to.''

"But what if they *do* catch on?" asked Jeremiah, filled with something of the foreboding of the ancient prophet whose name he bore.

"It won't 'appen," had said Coot firmly. "Never in a month of Sundays. It'd need more rotten luck than we got a right to expect. Listen, Jerry: in business, you got to take some chances. I'm more experienced than you. Just let me do the worryin' and be 'appy to take the money. That's all I ask."

So Jeremiah, borne down by Coot's arguments, and borne up by the prospect of income, agreed. All this had taken place a year ago, since when the two industrious apprentices had prospered exceedingly, being careful to transact their private business when their masters were out of town. It was for such opportunities that Coot and Jeremiah obeyed their masters more fully than they suspected, by watching out.

"Where shall we go tonight, Cooty?" asked Jeremiah, when he had ticketed and stowed away the cloak in his master's warehouse room.

"Ay raither fancy the Hopera," said Coot, with
extreme cultivation. "So get your rags on . . . and don't
forget your claret pot."

The pot referred to was Jeremiah's silver christening mug
that occupied, in his affections, a similar place to the great
silver timepiece in Coot's.

At a quarter past eight o'clock the two apprentices left
Henrietta Street for their night on the town. They marched
in step, as if an invisible band was playing—just for them.
They were smart, they were elegant, they were dapper.
They gladdened the heart and imparted a youthful gaiety
to the precincts of Bow Street. Their eyes sparkled, their
shoe-buckles twinkled, so there was brightness at both
ends, and money in the middle.

To begin with, they took in—as Coot put it—the second act of the opera. They went up into the gallery where, with footmen, students and other lively apprentices, they whistled and hooted and clapped, cheered on the lady performers and threw oranges down on bare heads in the pit till they were requested to leave or take the consequences. Then they went to a respectable inn and got mildly drunk on claret and port; after which Jeremiah was sick on the pavement and Coot fell into the snow. Partly recovered, they found a cock-fight in Feathers Court and lost ten shillings each on a bird that lay down before it was so much as tickled. Then they joined up with half a dozen weavers' apprentices and had a tremendous time trying to steal door-knockers and pelting a pursuing constable with stones disguised as snowballs.

They parted with the weavers' apprentices—who'd run out of money—and took up with a couple of likely lasses

who'd caught their roving eyes in the Strand. They told the girls they were soldiers on leave and that they'd been wounded in the foreign wars. They limped a bit to prove it . . . then kissed and cuddled and bought the girls supper in Maiden Lane, lording it over the waiter till the wretched man felt like pouring hot soup over the apprentices' heads.

But he did no such thing and Coot tipped him well to impress the girls with his careless generosity.

Coot and Jeremiah were firm believers in keeping business and pleasure apart. Though Coot would have fought with a cringing customer to the last breath in his body to beat him down by a shilling, he thought nothing at all of casting such a shilling (and two others like it) into the waiter's greasy palm. And Jeremiah who, with crocodile tears, would have denied a customer an extra penny, happily filled and refilled his silver tankard with wine, spilling it on the table and in his lap, at threepence a throw.

At last the two bright apprentices tottered back towards Drury Lane, quite worn out from their night on the town. They'd broken windows, tipped an old watchman into a horse-trough and unscrewed a lamp from a standing coach. They'd lost their lasses somewhere round the back of Covent Garden, and they'd not a penny left to bless themselves with; but they were happy and singing, and they kicked on front doors as they passed, with night-piercing screeches of "'appy Noo Year!"

"Look!" hiccuped Jeremiah, staring boozily down Drury Lane. "You got a customer, Cooty!"

Coot blinked and stared. Several figures seemed to be outside Mr Thompson's, and they were on fire; flames were coming up all round them. Coot wiped his eyes and the figures reduced themselves to two: a tall man and a link-boy who had, presumably, guided him there. The link-boy's torch leaped and danced and illuminated the three brass balls in a manner that was quite uncanny; the masks of Tragedy fairly glowered down.

Dazedly, Coot gazed upon the scene, then shouted out: "Shove off! We ain't open till eight o'clock!"

The customer saluted him, but did not move; so Coot pursued a winding, uncertain path to confront him and make his meaning clearer. The link-boy, seeing the angry apprentice, bolted and left the street to the feeble memory of his light.

"I told you," said Coot, squaring up to the customer in the manner of a weaving prizefighter, "we're shut. Closed. No business, see? All gone bye-bye. Shove off and come back in the mornin'."

The stranger, who was a good twelve inches taller than the pawnbroker's apprentice, looked down sombrely. There was something nasty about the man; he had a hooked nose like a vulture and eyes that seemed to keep shifting about all over his face. Coot took a step back, and bumped into Jeremiah, who had been sheltering behind him.

Suddenly the stranger reached into his pocket; and Coot, who was expecting a knife or a pistol, endeavoured to get behind his colleague. But the stranger only produced a slip of paper.

"Wassat?"

"Don't you recognize it?" inquired the stranger, harshly.

"'ow can I recko'nize it when you keeps wavin' it about?"

"It's a receipt."

"Reely? You don't say."

"It's a receipt for a cloak. You gave it to a gipsy woman this morning. She pawned the cloak with you for five shillings."

"Well, what of it?" said Coot valiantly. Events were moving a little too quickly for him quite to grasp their significance.

"It wasn't hers."

"Nicked? What an 'orrible thing. I'm sorry to 'ear it. Them gipsies! Night–night!"

"It was mine. I gave it out for cleaning. I can prove it was mine. There was a text inside the collar. 'I know that my Redeemer liveth.' I am that redeemer, my friend. I want my cloak back. Either that, or I fetch a magistrate to search your premises and examine your books. That's the law, my friend. So bring out the cloak."

Coot felt Jeremiah beside him begin to shake and tremble like a straw in a tempest. Although he couldn't see him, he knew his face had gone dead white and that he was crying; he always did.

But he, Coot, was made of sterner stuff; four weeks sterner. Delay, that was it. Put off the evil hour and it might never come to pass. There was no sense in meeting trouble half way. Far better to step aside and let it go rampaging past.

He informed the stranger that, at that precise moment, the cloak in question was in the firm's warehouse which, unfortunately, was some distance away. It couldn't be helped, and he, Coot, sympathised with the gent's annoyance. But that was how things were, and nothing was to be gained by crying over spilt milk. He would do his very best to obtain the garment in the course of a day or two. He couldn't speak fairer than that.

Just what was in Coot's complicated mind was hard to say. Perhaps he thought the stranger was a bad dream from which he would awaken if only given the time?

"I want my cloak now," said the stranger, refusing to behave like a dream. "Either that, or pay me the value of the garment. Ten pounds. The cloak, ten pounds—or the law."

At this point, Jeremiah spoke up. His voice fell upon the night like the wail of his namesake, the prophet, deploring the loss of Jerusalem.

"Give him the ten pound, Cooty! For God's sake, give him the ten pounds!"

The worst had happened, like he'd always known it would. The rotten luck that was more than they'd any right to expect, had befallen them. They were done for.

"And where am I goin' to get the ten pound?" snarled Coot, turning on his friend who retreated several paces, weeping bitterly.

"I don't know—I don't know!"

"Pardon me," said Coot to the stranger, who appeared to be relishing the friends' predicament. "Ay wish to consult with may colleague on business."

He joined Jeremiah.

"Keep your voice down!"

"Give him the ten pounds, then!"

"Can't. You give 'im the cloak."

"But I lent six pounds on it! How am I going to account for that? Old Long comes back the day after tomorrow!"

"So does old Thompson! And six pound is easier to find than ten."

"But I'll have to find it! You'll just be dropping me in it won't you Cooty?"

Coot laid a hand on Jeremiah's shoulder, as much to steady himself as to reassure his colleague.

"We're in it together, Jerry. We'll find a way. You just see if we don't. It'd take more rotten luck than we got a right to expect if we didn't manage some'ow. For Gawd's sake, Jerry, give 'im back the cloak!"

"You'll help, then?"

"I swear it. On me mother's grave," muttered Coot, forgetful of the fact that his mother was not yet in it. He returned to the stranger.

"We are sorry to 'ave hinconvenienced you," he said coldly, "but the garment was taken in good faith. We—I 'ad no idea the garment was nicked. 'owever, hunder the circs. we are prepared to return your property at no hextra charge. My colleague and I will—"

"At once!" interrupted the stranger, "or I go for the magistrate!"

"If you was a smaller man," said Coot venomously, "I'd punch you right in the nose!"

—⟨⟨⟨⟨⟨ ❋ ⟩⟩⟩⟩⟩—

"Six pounds!" wept Jeremiah. "How are we going to find it?" The cloak had been given up and the friends were still in Mr Long's shop.

"Don't you worry, Jerry," said Coot. "I'll come up with somethin'. I've never let you down yet."

"You've never had the chance!"

"Now that weren't friendly, Jerry. But I'll look after you."

37

"You'd better, Cooty. You'd better!"

"What do you mean by that?"

"If I go to jail, so do you. There's other things, you know. If I get caught on this one, you get caught on the others. Don't you think I'm going down alone. You always said we were in it together."

"That's nasty, Jerry. Particularly as you've always been 'appy to sit back and enjoy the money I thought of gettin'. But I don't 'old it against you. You're younger than me. All I want you to consider is that . . . well . . . what's the sense in both of us goin' down when it need only be one? Wouldn't it be better if one of us stayed safe so's 'e could 'elp the other when the time came?"

"All right. You take the blame and I'll help you when you come out of jail."

"Point taken," said Coot. "But the money 'appens to be missin' from your 'ouse, not mine. Otherwise I'd be 'appy to oblige."

Jeremiah began to cry again; then, seeing that his tears had no effect, grew exceedingly angry. He made it plain that he did not trust Coot. Coot had got him into it, and Coot was going to get him out. Or suffer by his side.

At last, Coot was forced to see how matters stood. Jeremiah was taking advantage of previous acts of friendship and was holding them against him. He just wasn't capable of distinguishing between business and pleasure.

"If that's the way it's to be," he said bitterly, "we got to lay our 'ands on six pounds; and another five shillin's, which is the hamount I'm in to Mr Thompson."

"And before the day after tomorrow," said Jeremiah,

anticipating any attempt to delay.

"Six pounds ain't a fortune," went on Coot, ignoring the interruption. "As I see it, there's reely only two ways of gettin' it. We could either borrer it—or nick it."

"I ain't stealing," said Jeremiah quickly. He felt that it was in Coot's mind for him, Jeremiah, to do the nicking. "You can get hung for that."

"Point taken," said Coot. "No nickin' on account of the risk. Although—"

"Any stealing you can do yourself, Cooty."

"Like I said, no nickin'. That leaves borrerin'."

"Who'd lend us six pounds, Cooty?"

"Good question. What about pawnin' more of the stock to each other?"

"I've had enough of that. We're sure to get found out."

Coot sighed and stared at his over-cautious associate. His eye fell upon Jeremiah's christening mug.

"All right," he said slowly. "Seein' as 'ow you've taken things out of my 'ands, you can do somethin' yourself for a change. 'ow about pawnin' that pot of yours?"

Jeremiah began to cry again. Tears ran out of his eyes as fast as melting snow. Contemptuously, Coot waited.

"You're a pig, Cooty," sobbed Jeremiah at length. "Take it, then; and give me the six pounds!"

"Six pounds?" said Coot. "Ay'm afraid," he began, from force of habit; and then corrected himself. "Climb down a bit, Jerry. You know I daren't make it six. Old Thompson goes through the books like a dog through a dust 'eap when 'e gets 'ome. 'e'd never stand for six pound! Not for an old piece of Sheffield plate with scratches all over it!"

"It's not plate! It's solid silver! I wasn't christened in plate!"

"Tell us another, Jerry! Look at it! Copper showin' through everywhere, plain as a baby's bum. Two pound is the very best. Solid silver my eye!"

"You're a dirty rotten liar, Cooty! Make it four pound, then?"

"I daren't, Jerry. It's more than me place is worth. Tell you what, though. I'll make it two pound ten shillin's and that'll only leave you three pound ten to find. There, now; don't say I ain't comin' up trumps. That's what I call real friendship!"

"And that's what I call dirty swindling, Cooty. You're not leaving here till all the money's made up. If you do, you be right in it alongside of me. You can pawn your watch . . ."

"Me timepiece?" cried Coot, shocked to the core. "But it's a valuable hobject. No . . . I couldn't do that."

"Then it's jail for the both of us."

"Do you know you're bein' very nasty, Jerry? And 'ard. I never thought you was so 'ard underneath."

"Your watch, Cooty. Come on. Let's have a look."

Silently Coot withdrew the gleaming article.

"This 'ere timepiece is worth—is worth fifteen pound if it's worth a penny," he said sorrowfully. "You're takin' an 'ammer to crack a egg, Jerry."

"Pass it over, Cooty."

Coot released his treasure from its chain and laid it on Jeremiah's counter. Jeremiah fell to examining it closely.

"Fifteen pound? Oh dear me, no! Old Long would have

me committed for life if I was to go along with that," said
Jeremiah. Like Coot, he had good reason to fear his
master's scrutiny of the books; and also he was still
smarting under Coot's treatment of his christening mug.

"If I was to give you two pounds, I'd be stretchin' it,
Cooty."

"Two pound? You dirty little skinflint!" shouted Coot,
banging on the counter so that the watch jumped in alarm.
Jeremiah folded his arms.

"To begin with," he said, "it ain't silver. It's only
pewter. And what's more, it's stopped ever since you
dropped it earlier on. And it's all scratched and dented like

a tinker's spoon. That there chain's worth more than the watch."

"That there timepiece was give me by my pa!" said Coot, savagely. "I wouldn't be pawnin' it but to 'elp *you*! Come on! Give us twelve pound!"

"You'll take two pound ten shillings," said Jeremiah coldly. "Just like me."

"You lousy rotten stinking little skinflint!" raged Coot, attempting to regain possession of his watch. "I'd sooner rot in jail than be treated like this! Oh for Gawd's sake, Jerry, make it nine pound and call it a day? Please, Jerry! It's me pa's watch! It's valuable to me . . . It—it's all I got in the world!"

"Two pound ten," said Jeremiah. "Less warehousing, of course."

"You're cuttin' off your own nose, Jerry. You're cuttin' your own throat."

"And yours, Cooty," said Jeremiah, not without satisfaction.

"What about the other pound and five shillin's?"

"I'll take your weskit for half of it; and you can take my new coat for the rest. That's fair."

"Your coat, Jerry, it pains me to tell you, ain't worth more'n two shillin's. I'll 'ave your best shoes, too!"

"I don't like you, Cooty."

"Nor me you, Jerry. And I never 'ave."

Following on this frightful revelation, there was a longish pause.

"But it's been worth it," said Jeremiah, finally. He had been brooding on how he might display, even more

crushingly, his contempt for Coot. "Yes. I don't begrudge the experience. It's shown you up, Cooty. I'm glad to have paid to see you, really to see you. I've had a narrow escape, Cooty. I might have turned out like you, if I hadn't seen what you're like underneath."

"Likewise," said Coot, determined to outdo Jeremiah. "And what's more, I'd willin'ly 'ave paid out double to see what I 'ave just seen. 'orrible. Made me sick to me stomach. You're the sort, Jerry, what gets 'uman bein's a bad name. Thank Gawd I found out in time."

Jeremiah, who could come up with nothing better for the moment, opened the shop door and indicated that his colleague's presence was no longer welcome. Breathing heavily, the two apprentices stood in the doorway. Coot thought of punching Jeremiah in the face. He shook his head. He recollected, "Vengeance is mine; I will repay, saith the Lord." He stared up and saw the weighty emblem of Mr Long's trade poised above Jeremiah's head. "Go on, God!" he thought. "Fix 'im!" But the three brass balls remained stolidly in the air.

"And don't you go sending me any of your customers any more," said Jeremiah, having thought of something else. "Because I'll tell them what a grinding little skinflint you are. I'll show you up. If you send them to me, I'll give them what they ask for."

"And I'll give 'em more!" said Coot furiously. "Just for the pleasure of hexposin' you! I wouldn't send a dog to you, Jerry!"

"If I could find that gipsy," quavered Jeremiah, stung to the quick; "I'd get down on my hands and knees and thank her for letting me see the truth."

"I might remind you," said Coot loftily, "that I'm the one she came to. I'm the one what was chosen to be redeemed."

Jeremiah breathed deeply.

"Garn!" he said. "You don't know the meaning of the word!"

Slowly Coot made his way back to Drury Lane. A church clock began to strike midnight; the New Year was past. Unthinkingly Coot fumbled for his watch to see if the church was right. No watch; no waistcoat, even. He shivered as he felt the cold strike through.

Snow had begun to fall again: tiny flakes that pricked and glittered as they passed through the feeble rays of the street lamps. Little by little, as the snow settled, the black scars and furrows that marked the road lost their sharpness and seemed to fade. Presently they were reduced to smudgy ghosts, like rubbed out entries in a ledger.

By the time he reached Drury Lane, the snow was fairly whirling down and he was as white as the street. The flakes kept stinging him in the eyes so that he could scarcely see where he was going.

It was under these circumstances that he saw the apparition; and considering how much he'd drunk and what he'd been through, it wasn't surprising. He saw the Holy Family.

Out of the snow they came: the laden donkey, the radiant mother and the tall, saintly man beside her. Coot crossed himself as they drew near.

"Buy an apple, dear!" called out the gipsy woman. "Buy a sweet Kent apple for good luck!"

"A happy New Year! A happy New Year, my boy!" called out the man by her side.

He was the stranger, the hook-nosed stranger, stalking along in his treacherous, ruinous black silk cloak!

They'd been in it together—the pair of them! They'd done him! They'd swindled him! They'd stripped him bare! The thieves! The rogues! The rotten, crafty swindlers! They were all in it . . . most likely the baby and the donkey, too!

Coot stood as still as a post; and then began to shake and tremble with indignation. Helplessly he watched them pass him by and then vanish like a dream into the whirling curtain of snow.

Then he gathered together his tattered shreds of self-respect and reflected on many things.

"I suppose it were worth it," he whispered. "All things considered, I suppose it were worth it in the end."

With aching head and shaking hands, he unlocked the door of Mr Thompson's (Personal Banking upon Moderate Terms), and let himself in.

He leaned across the counter, staring into the dark emptiness, which was his place in life.

"If anybody comes in to pawn a soul," he whispered, remembering his master's little joke, "just you send 'em down to Mr Long's! But what if," he went on, smiling mournfully to himself, "they comes in to redeem one?"

He went to the door again and opened it. He stared out

46

into the teeming weather. Although the little family had long since gone, he fancied he saw them imprinted on the ceaseless white. He tried to recollect their features—the man, the woman, the tiny child. But they were just shapes, haunting shapes that left no footprints; all that remained was a vague perfume of apples and spice.

"Try my colleague in 'enrietta Street," he called softly into the night. "Go on; try Mister Jeremiah, my friend."